101 DALMATIANS

Once upon a time, there was a Dalmatian named Pongo. He lived in London with his owner, Roger.

Roger was an unmarried songwriter-composer who led a carefree life, like Pongo… until one memorable spring day.

Pongo was looking out the window when he saw the most beautiful lady Dalmatian he had ever seen! She was walking toward the park with her owner. Pongo decided that they would make the perfect couple. After all, it was about time that he and Roger found lady friends!

Pongo picked up his leash and barked until Roger agreed to take him to the park. The lady and her Dalmatian were seated on the edge of a pond, but Roger didn't even notice them!

To get the other dog's attention, Pongo wrapped his leash around Roger and the lady until they were all tangled up. They lost their balance, falling into the pond with a splash! As they got out of the water, Pongo was relieved to see that they were both smiling and laughing.

Just as Pongo had hoped, Roger and the lady fell in love. It wasn't long before Roger and Anita were married.

Anita, Perdita, and Nanny the housekeeper moved in with Roger. Soon after that, Perdita and Pongo welcomed fifteen little puppies.

That's when an evil lady named Cruella De Vil paid a visit to their home. The spoiled and rich woman was an old schoolmate of Anita's. She blew into the house like a tornado, waving her checkbook and pen.

Ink splattered all over Roger's face and clothing. She demanded that Roger sell her all the puppies.

"They're not for sale," Roger replied firmly. "Not even one!"

One night, two suspicious men knocked on the door.

"We work for the electric company," they lied.

Their names were Horace and Jasper. Cruella had sent them to steal the pups. Nanny tried to get rid of them, but they took off with the puppies.

While the humans were busy calling the police, Pongo and Perdita took action. They spread the terrible news using the "Twilight Bark," a canine version of the telephone. Dogs throughout the town barked the message from house to house until it reached their cousins in the countryside. Every dog in town was now searching for the stolen pups.

At last, the message reached an old sheepdog named Colonel, a horse named Captain, and a cat named Sergeant Tibs. Tibs had heard a dog barking in the lot next door—the abandoned lot that belonged to Cruella!

Sergeant Tibs snuck into the house. He was shocked to find ninety-nine Dalmatians!

He could hear Cruella De Vil yelling, "I want my new fur coat!"

Horrified, Sergeant Tibs hid the dogs under a staircase.

Thankfully, Pongo and Perdita arrived just in time! Growling and
baring their teeth, the two dogs distracted Horace and Jasper, while
Sergeant Tibs led the puppies out of the house.

When Pongo and Perdita learned of Cruella's terrible plan, they didn't hesitate to save all ninety-nine puppies. A violent snowstorm was brewing and the Dalmatians were forced to trudge through the icy snow.

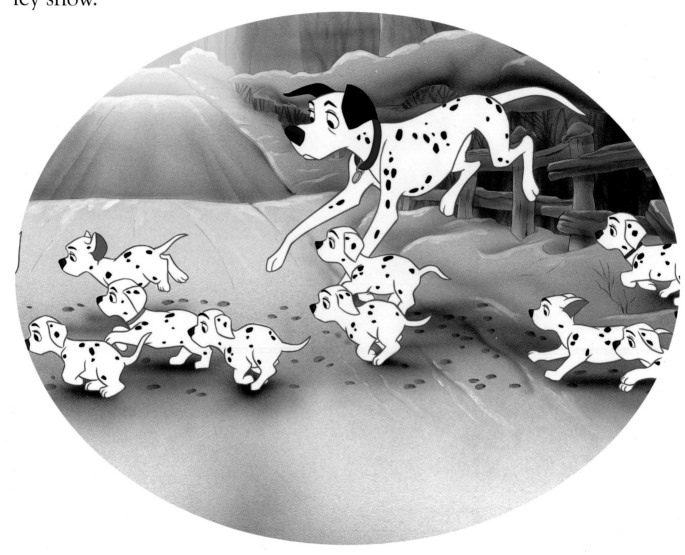

They found food and shelter in a nearby dairy stable. The cows generously offered their visitors warm milk and everyone took shelter from the cold outside.

The next day, the group met a kind Labrador who told them about a truck that would soon be leaving for London. The truck was parked in the street, but before the Dalmatians could reach it, Cruella arrived.

A few of the pups had been playing in black soot and had become very dirty. Pongo had an idea.

"Everyone roll in the soot," he said. "Then we'll all look like Labradors!"

One by one, Pongo and Perdita helped the little black pups cross the road.

Their plan was working until Lucky, the last puppy, reached the truck. The melting snow had washed his soot away, revealing his spotted coat. Cruella saw Lucky, but the truck started down the road before she could reach it.

"Follow that truck!" cried Cruella to Horace and Jasper, as they hopped into their car. Cruella got into her own car and sped dangerously down the slippery road.

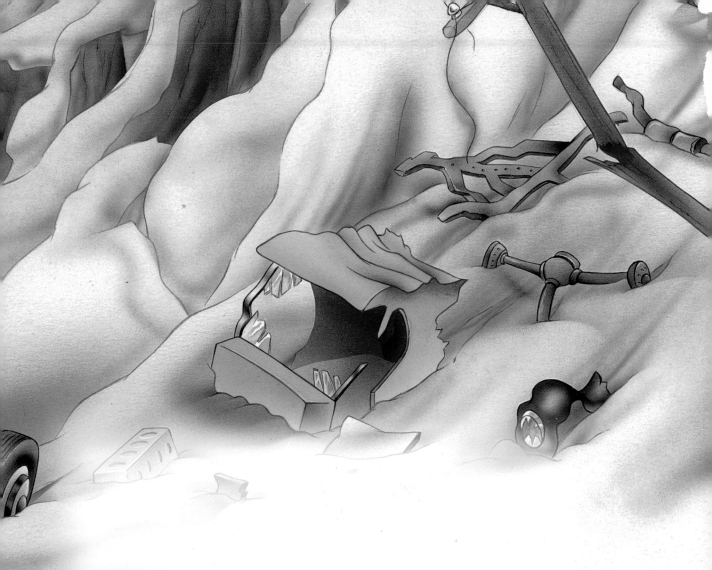

As Horace and Jasper tried to block the truck's route, they plowed into Cruella's car! The two cars veered off the road and into a snowbank while the truck continued down the road toward London.

Soon, the puppies were safe and sound at Roger's house.
Nanny was thrilled to see the dogs.

"One, two…" she counted as she dusted them off one by one.
"Ninety-nine… one-hundred-and-one Dalmatians!"

Roger and Anita were thrilled to have the dogs home again.
Roger played a song he had written about moving to a big home in the
country, where they could all live together. And that's exactly what they did!